This book belongs to

For Tim and Emily
with love
– P. L.

For Aaron
– P. I.

tiger tales

5 River Road, Suite 128, Wilton, CT 06897
This edition published in the United States 2013
First published in the United States 2002
Originally published in Great Britain 2000
by Little Tiger Press Ltd.
Text copyright © 2000 Paeony Lewis
Illustrations copyright © 2000 Penny Ives
ISBN-13: 978-1-58925-441-1
ISBN-10: 1-58925-441-4
Printed in the United States
20 19 18 17 16 15 14 13 12

For more insight and activities,
visit us at www.tigertalesbooks.com

I'll Always Love You

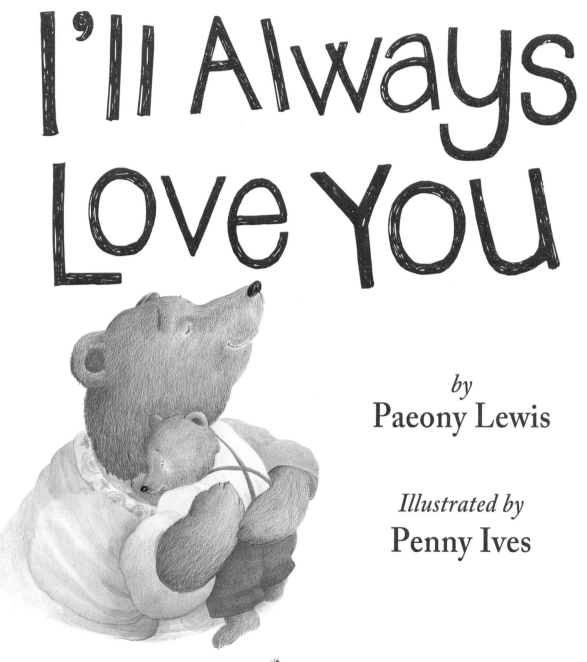

by
Paeony Lewis

Illustrated by
Penny Ives

tiger tales

One morning Alex woke up early and ran downstairs to the kitchen. "I'll make Mom some toast and honey for breakfast," he said. "She'll like that."

Alex reached for the honey bowl and...

CRASH!

His mom's favorite bowl was
now nine pieces of sticky china.

Alex hadn't *meant* to break it. What would she say?

Alex's mom was doing her morning exercises. "Hello, Alex," she said. "Did I hear something break?"

"Mom, will you only love me if I'm good?" asked Alex.

"I'll always love you," said his mom, and she smiled.

"Even when I've done something that isn't good?" asked Alex.

"I'll still love you," said his mom. "Honest."

"What if I have a pillow fight with Joey Bear and all the feathers burst out? Will you still love me?"

"I'll always love you. Though you must pick up all the feathers."

"What if I spill my new paints on Baby Pog and she turns green, red, and blue? Will you still love me?"

"I'll always love you. Though you will have to give her a bath."

"What if I forget to close the fridge door and Baby Pog pulls everything out? Will you still love me?"

"I'll always love you. Though there won't be any food for dinner."

"What if I pour Grandma Bear's lumpy oatmeal all over my head? Will you still love me?"

"I'll always love you. Though you will have to eat another bowl of oatmeal. Now, why are you being such a silly bear this morning?"

For a few moments Alex didn't say anything. Then he whispered, "What if I break your favorite honey bowl? Will you still love me?"

"You know I'll always love you," said his mom. "Come on, Alex. It must be time for breakfast."

And off they went into the kitchen.

"Oh no!" cried his mom when she saw the nine pieces of sticky china. "That was my favorite bowl, Alex."

"Sorry," said Alex. Two tears ran down his face. "You said you would still love me. I love you."

"Of course I love you," said Alex's mom, hugging him.

"Hey, I've got an idea!" shouted Alex, wriggling from her arms.

"What is it?" she asked.

"It's a surprise," Alex said and he ran off to his bedroom.

He looked in his toy box ...

he looked in his closet ...

and he looked under his table.

At last he found what he wanted.

He got out his new paints, poured some water into a jelly jar, and swirled his paintbrush around.

A little while later, Alex came downstairs again. "Here you are, Mom," he said. "But be careful, the paint's still wet."

"I'll be very careful," said his mom, smiling. "Because this is going to be my new favorite honey bowl!"

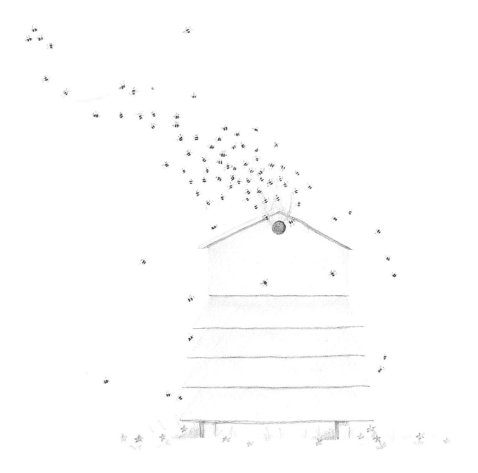